WHEN YOU ARE ANXIOUS

Zoe's Hiding Place

DAVID POWLISON

Editor

JOE HOX

Illustrator

Story creation by Jocelyn Flenders, a homeschooling mother, writer, and editor living in suburban Philadelphia. A graduate of Lancaster Bible College with a background in intercultural studies and counseling, the Good News for Little Hearts series is her first published work for children.

New Growth Press, Greensboro, NC 27404
Text copyright © 2018 by David Powlison
Illustration copyright © 2018 by New Growth Press

Cover/Interior Design and Typesetting: Trish Mahoney, themahoney.com
Cover/Interior Illustrations: Joe Hox, joehox.com

ISBN: 978-1-948130-23-3

Library of Congress Cataloging-in-Publication Data
Names: Powlison, David, 1949- author.
Title: Zoe's hiding place : when you are anxious / David Powlison.
Description: Greensboro : New Growth Press, 2018. | Series: Good news for little hearts
Identifiers: LCCN 2018043738 | ISBN 9781948130233 (trade cloth)
Subjects: LCSH: Anxiety--Religious aspects--Christianity--Juvenile literature. | Fear--Religious aspects--Christianity--Juvenile literature.
Classification: LCC BV4908.5 .P693 2018 | DDC 242/.62--dc23
LC record available at https://lccn.loc.gov/2018043738

Printed in Canada

25 24 23 22 21 20 19 18   2 3 4 5 6

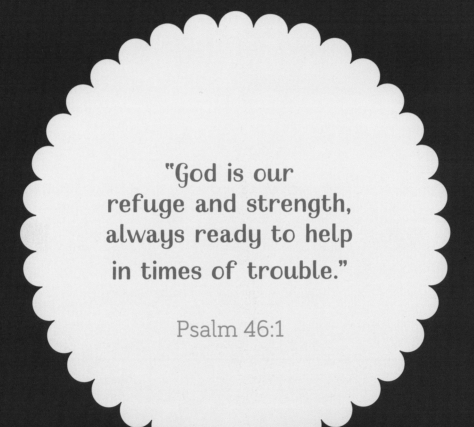

"God is our
refuge and strength,
always ready to help
in times of trouble."

Psalm 46:1

The sun extended its morning glow to a light blue bungalow in Mulberry Meadow.

"Zoe!" called Mama,
"It's time for breakfast!"

Zoe Mouse peeked out from under her purple patchwork quilt.
"This is my favorite place to hide. I feel so safe and cozy.
No worries here!"

"Zoe!"
Mama called again,
"It's time
for breakfast!"

Finally she jumped out of bed, dressed, and smoothed her long pink tail.
Then collecting her backpack and her favorite book of fairy tales she
pattered down the hallway, as quiet as a mouse, to join Papa, Mama, and baby Zack.

"Good morning!"
she beamed.

"Good morning, Zoe!"
replied Papa.

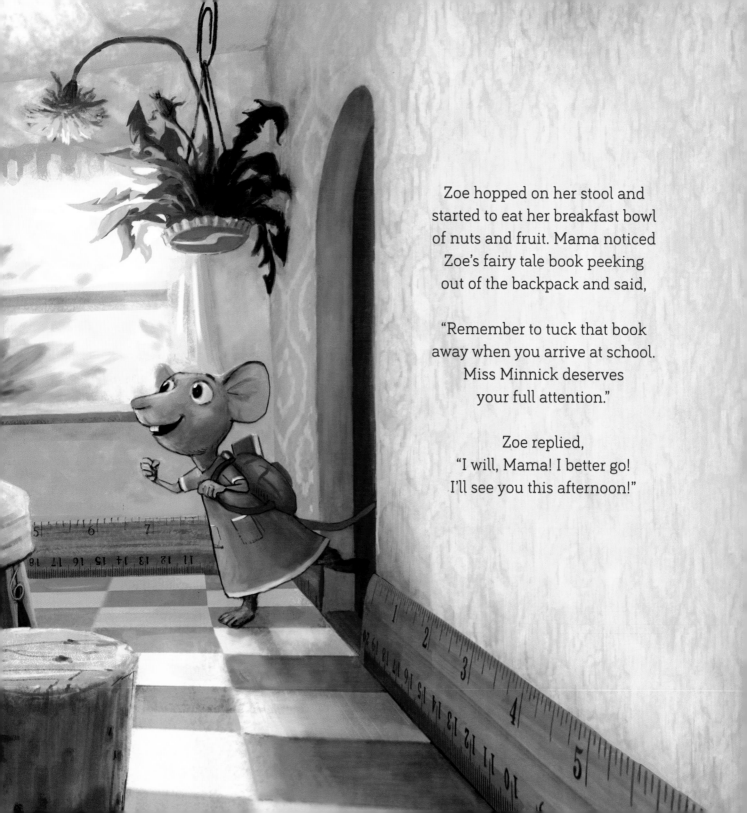

Zoe hopped on her stool and started to eat her breakfast bowl of nuts and fruit. Mama noticed Zoe's fairy tale book peeking out of the backpack and said,

"Remember to tuck that book away when you arrive at school. Miss Minnick deserves your full attention."

Zoe replied,
"I will, Mama! I better go! I'll see you this afternoon!"

With the long walk to school before her, Zoe was free to dive into her book. She read a little, then walked a little, read and walked, imagining each and every detail. She barely noticed her friend, Layla, joining her along the way.

Layla interrupted Zoe's thoughts
with her usual string of how do you do's.
"Good morning, Zoe! What are you reading?
Would you like to sit together in class?"

Zoe happily replied,
"It's my new favorite fairy tale!

I'm trying to finish it by the end of the day.
And, yes, I'd love to sit together in class!"

The girls entered through the thicket to where they gathered
for school. They hung their bags on some handy branches and sat down
on a carpet of clover, waiting for Miss Minnick to start the school day.

"Good morning, class!" said Miss Minnick. "I have a special announcement!
The Mulberry Meadow Art Museum has invited us back for a visit!
We will leave first thing tomorrow morning."

Layla turned to Zoe and whispered,
"Isn't tomorrow going to be terrific! I can hardly wait!"
Waking up from her daydream, Zoe asked, "Hardly wait for what?"

"Didn't you hear what Miss Minnick said?
We're going to the art museum tomorrow! I won't
be able to think of anything else for the rest of the day!"

Zoe sighed. "Great."
But Zoe didn't feel great.

On her last trip to the art museum there was a painting that reminded her of her favorite
fairy tale. She was so busy looking that she didn't notice the class leaving. When she
looked up, she didn't know what to do or where to go.

"IT FELT LIKE I WAS ALONE FOREVER.
I never want to go to that museum again!" she thought.

Walking home after school,
Zoe's mind filled with worries.

She tried to read her fairy tale book,
but thoughts of lonely rooms and
scary pictures filled her mind.

As Zoe neared home, she was filled with
FEAR and WORRY.

Once inside, Zoe hurried past Mama and Zack. She headed straight to her bedroom to be alone under her safe, purple quilt. After a few minutes, Mama ventured down the hall to check on her. Zoe peeked out from under her quilt and slowly began to share her worries with Mama.

Mama had good listening ears. She said, "Every mouse experiences worry. And I can certainly understand why you feel anxious.

WE DO REMEMBER TROUBLE. WE IMAGINE IT COULD HAPPEN AGAIN.

We get scared and anxious. We want to keep safe. That's how God made us. It sounds like you might want to stay home from the field trip?"

Zoe nodded her head yes.

Mama continued, "Worry wants you to believe that you are all alone and God isn't with you to protect you.

But, that's not true. Jesus is with you. He cares for you.
I had lots of fears and worries when I was a young mouse. Your Grandpa used to read to me from the Great Book. There is a verse in that book that says,

'GOD IS YOUR REFUGE—A SAFE PLACE FROM TROUBLE AND FEAR.'

That verse is true! You can trust God to keep you safe."

"God kind of reminds me of my purple quilt,"
squeaked Zoe from under her quilt.

"Yes, but so much better," Mama replied.
"God is always with us. Another place in the Great Book says,

'I WILL NEVER LEAVE YOU OR FORSAKE YOU, YOU ARE MINE.'"

"So that means even though
I can't see God he is here?" said Zoe.

"Yes," said Mama.

"Wherever you go Jesus is with you. I still have worries too. But I ask Jesus for help. You can't change tomorrow by worrying. But you can tell Jesus your worries.

TURN EACH FEAR INTO A PRAYER. HE WILL HELP YOU.

"And don't forget how important it is to listen carefully to the people in charge of keeping you safe. Some of your worry might be helped if you put on your listening ears when Miss Minnick is talking."

The next day, Zoe awoke. During the night, scary thoughts had filled her mind. But Zoe remembered her talk with her mom. "Jesus is with me. Jesus wants to help."

Zoe prayed, "Jesus, I know I have trouble listening and paying attention. I am worried that today at the museum I will not listen and get lost.

I'm so afraid. Please help me."

As Zoe was leaving for school, Papa gave her a slip of paper with words from the Great Book. She tucked the verse in her pocket.

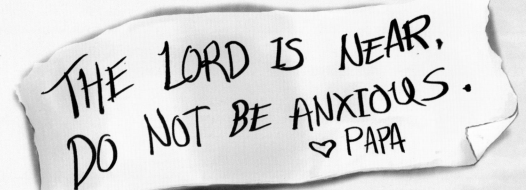

Papa gave her a kiss and reminded her,
"Pull it out and read it when you feel afraid."

On the path to school, instead of worrying,
Zoe noticed how many shades of green were in God's world.
And she didn't feel so alone. She knew that God was with her,
and she felt his peace.

Suddenly Layla ran up exclaiming,
"Off we go! I'm so excited! I could hardly sleep last night."

She took Zoe's hand and together they ran the rest of the way to the school and fell into line with the rest of the class already waiting to leave for the Mulberry Meadow Art Museum.

When they arrived at the museum, Zoe took a deep breath and prayed, "God, help me to pay attention.

Thank you for your listening ears. Thank you for never leaving me."

The Great Oak Tree guarding the entrance to the museum invited them in. The class walked into a room that Zoe had never visited. She was enthralled!

"There is so much to see! In all my worry, I forgot how much I love the art museum."

Each painting was from a fairy tale. Zoe's favorite was the mural of the mouse and the elephant. She imagined being the brave mouse, courageously approaching the enormous elephant. Lost in the painting, Zoe didn't notice the rest of the class leaving.

Zoe remembered.
She reached into her pocket and pulled out the note.

"THE LORD IS NEAR."

Zoe prayed right then and there, "I'm sorry for not paying attention.
I'm listening Lord. Thank you for being near. Please help me to know what to do."

Then she remembered that all she had to do was find the Great Oak at the beginning of the meadow. She walked out of the gallery and saw the Great Oak and her class in the distance. As she ran toward them, she heard her friends laughing and talking as they ate lunch under the trees.

Miss Minnick saw her and exclaimed,
"Zoe, there you are!
I am so glad to see you! I must do a better
job keeping you with the class.
Are you okay, my dear?"

Zoe replied,
"YES, I am, thank you.
I'm so sorry for not following you and the class.
I am learning to have listening ears.
And Miss Minnick, I am more than okay!
I'm learning a lot
on this field trip!"

Helping Your Child with Anxiety

The best way to help your child is for you to know how God "comforts us in all our troubles so we can comfort others" (2 Corinthians 1:4). As you talk with your child about anxiety, ask the Lord to be teaching you at the same time how to trust him in a world of troubles. Then you can share with your child the comfort you receive. Here are some things to remember that will bring comfort to you and your child in the midst of fear and anxiety.

1 **We have good reasons to be anxious and afraid.** Stress and anxiety are universal human struggles. We live in a broken world where things can and do go wrong. On our own we don't have the power to fix others, our world, or ourselves. Your children may not be able to articulate these truths, but they do feel them—just as you do. Jesus acknowledges this when he reminds his disciples (and us) that in this world we will have trouble (John 16:33).

2 **The most frequent command in the Bible is "Don't be afraid."** God knows our human tendency to be fearful and he responds by telling us not to fear. This is not a command with a warning attached to disobeying it (like the Ten Commandments). It's a command with promises attached to it. It's those promises that you can remember and share with your child.

3 **The Lord gives us better reasons for trusting him.** God, in his Word, gives us imperishable reasons (promises) for responding to the troubles of life with faith. You can learn to remember that God is near in the midst of trouble (Philippians 4:5–6). You can learn to remember that he is our refuge and strength, a very present help in times of trouble (Psalm 46:1). You can teach your child to remember these things as well.

4 **Help your child identify the source of anxiety.** Zoe's mom had "listening ears." Just as God listens to our troubles, Zoe's mom listened and heard what Zoe was afraid of and understood how Zoe wanted to deal with her fears.

5 **Remind your child that the Lord has listening ears.** Because the Lord is near, he is also listening to us. "I love the LORD because he hears my voice" (Psalm 116:1). Encourage your children to tell God specifically about the troubles that are filling their minds and hearts. Pray with and for them.

6 **Remind your child that the Lord is speaking to them about their fears.** Think with your child about what God says to us when we are anxious. Remember with them that Jesus is with them and will never leave them (Hebrews 13:5). Perhaps you have some favorite Bible verses you can remind them of when they are anxious. Here are some of mine:

> *"The Lord is near. Don't worry about anything; instead, pray about everything. Tell God what you need, and thank him for all he has done" (Philippians 4:5–6).*

> *"Give all your worries and cares to God, for he cares about you" (1 Peter 5:7).*

> *"The LORD keeps you from all harm and watches over your life. The LORD keeps watch over you as you come and go, both now and forever" (Psalm 121:7–8).*

> *"The LORD is my shepherd; I have all that I need" (Psalm 23:1).*

7 **Look for specific ways to help your child remember what God says to them when they are afraid.** Papa gave Zoe a verse to put into her pocket—a very concrete way for a child (or anyone!) to remember God's promise of help in the midst of trouble. You can use the Bible verses at the end of the book as a way to help you and your child remember when you are anxious that the Lord is near. Or think of other ways to help. Perhaps post a Bible promise somewhere for your whole family to see or even memorizing a psalm together (Psalm 23 and 121 are short and full of comfort for worried children and adults).

8 **Notice God's world with your child.** Jesus encourages us to consider the beauty of the lilies and God's care for even the smallest bird (Matthew 6:25–33). As Zoe walked to school, she noticed God's world around her. Being out in God's world reminds us that God is bigger than us and cares for us.

9 **Encourage your child to say "sorry" to God and others when appropriate.** Zoe struggled to listen. And when she didn't listen she got lost. She did need to say "sorry" to Miss Minnick. God is faithful to forgive all who say "sorry" because Jesus died for our sins (1 John 1:7—2:2). Remind your child that asking and receiving forgiveness is just an everyday part of life as God's child.

10 **Encourage your child to take one small step of faith and love.** For Zoe that was going on the trip to the museum even though she was afraid. What small, constructive thing might you encourage your child to do today?

Back Pocket Bible Verses

The Lord is near. Don't worry about anything; instead, pray about everything. Tell God what you need, and thank him for all he has done.

Philippians 4:5-6

Give all your worries and cares to God, for he cares about you.

1 Peter 5:7

The Lord keeps you from all harm and watches over your life. The Lord keeps watch over you as you come and go, both now and forever.

Psalm 121:7-8

The Lord is my shepherd; I have all that I need.

Psalm 23:1

Back Pocket Bible Verses

WHEN YOU ARE ANXIOUS

WHEN YOU ARE ANXIOUS

GOOD NEWS FOR LITTLE HEARTS

GOOD NEWS FOR LITTLE HEARTS

WHEN YOU ARE ANXIOUS

WHEN YOU ARE ANXIOUS

GOOD NEWS FOR LITTLE HEARTS

GOOD NEWS FOR LITTLE HEARTS